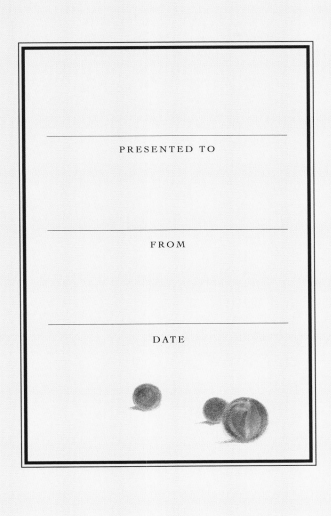

PRESENTED TO

_____

FROM

_____

DATE

To the Questioning Child

———

ABOUT THE AUTHOR AND ILLUSTRATOR

BARBARA J. PORTER teaches English at Bountiful High School in Utah. She has a Masters in Education from Weber State University. She and her husband are the parents of three grown children and anxiously await the time when they'll be answering questions for their grandchildren.

DILLEEN MARSH is an artist who lives and works in Salt Lake City, Utah. Her work has appeared in such varied places as the Friend magazine, Franklin Covey business publications, and a book used to raise funds for refugees of the Bosnian conflict in conjunction with the Graham Crusade. She and her husband have two children.

Text copyright © 1992 by Barbara J. Porter
Illustrations copyright © 1992 by Dilleen Marsh

Library of Congress Cataloging-in-Publication Data

Porter, Barbara J., 1946–
   [All kinds of answers]
   Some answers are loud, some answers are soft / written by Barbara
J. Porter ; illustrated by Dilleen Marsh.
     p.   cm.
   Summary: Explores different kinds of questions and answers,
including answers to prayers.
   ISBN 1-57345-557-1
   [1. Questions and answers Fiction.]   I. Marsh, Dilleen, 1952–
ill. II. Title.
PZ7.P817So   1999
[E]—dc21
                                    99-28393
                                      CIP

Printed in Mexico   18961-6488
10 9 8 7 6 5 4 3 2 1

Some Answers
Are Loud
Some Answers
Are Soft

Written by
Barbara J. Porter

Illustrated by
Dilleen Marsh

SHADOW MOUNTAIN

Some answers are loud—
like when you ask your mom
if you can have a pet snake.

Some answers are soft—
like when you ask the
librarian where the books
on dinosaurs are.

Some answers don't make any noise at all—like when you ask, "Can I get in bed with you?" and your parents scoot over to make a place just your size between them.

Some answers make you feel lonely—like when you ask your best friend to come over, and he says he's playing with someone else.

Some answers make you feel excited—like when you ask, "Where are we going Monday night?" and your parents say,
"To the zoo!"

Some answers aren't answers at all—like when you ask, "Is it time for recess?" and the teacher says, "It's not your turn to talk."

Some answers are questions—like when you ask, "May I stay up a little later?" and your mom says, "Have you brushed your teeth?"

Some answers
make you feel
embarrassed —
like when you
ask your friend

if you can play with
his marbles, and he
says, "No! Last time
you lost my best
shooter."

And some answers make you feel proud—like when you ask, "What did I get on the spelling test?" and your teacher says, "You got every one right!"

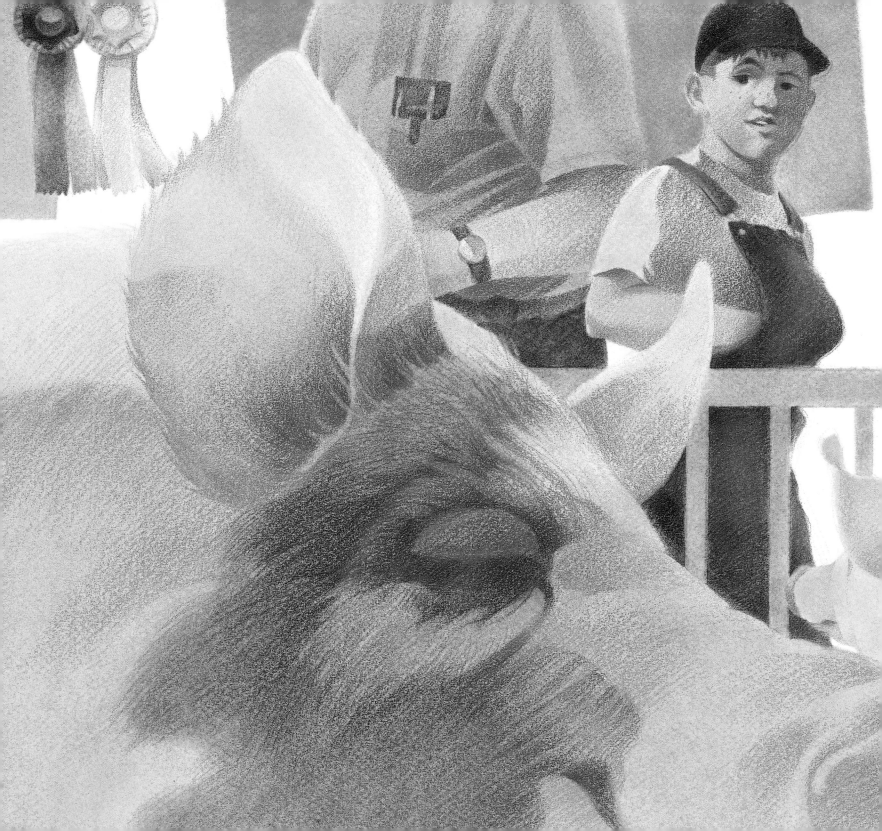

Some answers are silly—like if you ask, "When can we get a motorcycle?" and your dad says, "When pigs fly!"

And some answers are serious—
like when you ask what happens
to birds when they die.

Some answers make you feel kind of scared—like when you ask if it will hurt, and the doctor says, "Maybe a little."

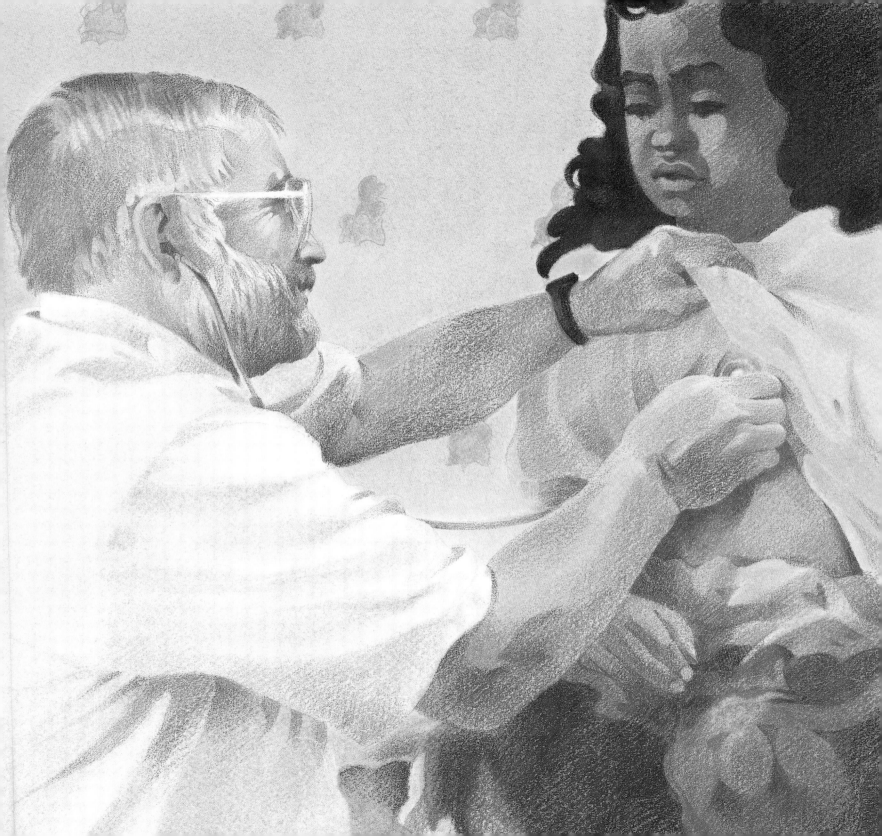

And some answers make you feel safe—like when you ask your mom if she'll stay with you, and she says, "Of course I will."

And sometimes you need answers that only your Heavenly Father knows. You can hear him when you're very still and listen with your heart.

His are the very best answers of all.